DODSWORTH

Written and illustrated by

TIM EGAN

Green Light Readers

HOUGHTON MIFFLIN HARCOURT

BOSTON   NEW YORK

For all my friends and family in Colorado.

For information about permission to reproduce selections from this book,
write to Permissions, Houghton Mifflin Harcourt Publishing Company,
215 Park Avenue South, New York, New York 10003.

www.hmhco.com

The text of this book is set in Cochin.
The illustrations are ink and watercolor on paper.

Library of Congress Cataloging-in-Publication Data:
Egan, Tim, 1957–
Dodsworth in Tokyo/by Tim Egan.
p. cm.
Summary: Dodsworth's duck companion is surprisingly well-behaved
during a visit to Tokyo, although he does fall into a koi pond at the
Imperial Palace and becomes the center of attention at a Sanja Festival.
[1.Voyages and travels—Fiction. 2. Tokyo (Japan)—Fiction.
3. Japan—Fiction. 4. Ducks—Fiction.] Title.
PZ7.E2815Dot 2013
[E]—dc23
2012034049

ISBN: 978-0-547-87745-7 hardcover
ISBN: 978-0-544-33915-6 paperback

Manufactured in China
SCP 10 9 8 7 6 5 4 3 2 1

4500478249

CONTENTS

CHAPTER ONE
LAND OF THE RISING SUN

The plane glided over Mount Fuji.

Tokyo sparkled in the distance.

Dodsworth was a little nervous.

Japan is a land of customs and

manners and order.

The duck wasn't very good at those things.

"We should be on our best behavior here," said Dodsworth.

"Will do," said the duck.

Dodsworth had heard that before.

"Arigato," he said to the duck.

"That means 'thank you.'"

The duck nodded.

Dodsworth was still nervous.

The plane landed safely at the Narita airport.
As they passed through customs, Dodsworth
bowed to the guard.

"Why did you do that?" asked the duck.

"It's how you greet people here," said
Dodsworth. "It's a sign of respect."

They walked through the airport.

The duck bowed at everyone they passed.

After a few minutes, he started getting dizzy.

Dodsworth smiled.

"You don't have to bow to everybody," he

said. The duck was relieved to hear that.

They took a train to a hotel in Shibuya.

Bright neon signs lit up the crowded streets.

The duck was so busy looking at the signs,

he bumped into a rickshaw carrying tourists.

The rickshaw driver stopped suddenly and

the tourists almost fell out.

"Oops," said the duck.

"Unbelievable," said Dodsworth.

The driver shouted at the duck in Japanese.
The duck had no idea what he was saying,
but it didn't sound good.
The rickshaw pulled away.
"Listen," said Dodsworth. "For some reason,
trouble follows you everywhere, so you have
to be careful and pay attention. Understand?"
The duck nodded.

That evening, they walked through Yoyogi Park.

A gardener was trimming little bonsai trees.

Some folks were practicing karate.

A little girl was playing with a wooden toy.

She was trying to get a ball onto a stick.

"That's a kendama," said Dodsworth.

The duck liked the kendama.

They stopped at a restaurant.

Dodsworth started taking off his shoes.

"Now what are you doing?" asked the duck.

"You remove your shoes when entering a

place," said Dodsworth. "It's a custom."

The duck never wore shoes.

He thought it was a good custom.

They ordered sushi for dinner.

The duck had always loved sushi.

He ate every last piece.

After dinner, the waitress said to

Dodsworth, "*Arigato*. Your duck is very

well behaved."

Nobody had ever said that about the

duck before.

As they walked back through the park,
Dodsworth said, "I'm very proud of you.
You didn't throw food or anything."
"I never throw sushi," said the duck.
They passed by a bench and saw the
kendama.
"Uh-oh," said the duck. "That girl forgot
her toy."

"Maybe she'll come back," said Dodsworth.
"Let's wait here for a little while."
"Can we play with it?" asked the duck.
"Sure," said Dodsworth. "Now, you're
supposed to get the ball onto the stick or
into the cup."
Dodsworth couldn't get the ball to do either.
"It's harder than it looks," he said.

Then the duck tried. He got the ball onto
the stick nine times straight.

Dodsworth was very impressed.

The duck played with it for another hour.

"It's getting late," said Dodsworth. "Let's
bring it back in the morning. Maybe we'll
find the girl."

The duck liked that idea.

CHAPTER TWO
WAGASHI

The next morning, they passed a window
filled with colorful treats.

"Those are wagashi," said Dodsworth.

"They're Japanese desserts. We'll get
some later."

The duck was delighted to hear that.

He loved dessert.

They arrived at the bench in the park.
The area was packed with tourists.
They looked for the little girl but didn't
see her.
"I don't want to leave the kendama here,"
said Dodsworth. "Let's go sightseeing.
We'll come back this afternoon."

They took a tour of Tokyo.

They drove past the Tokyo Tower
and through the Ginza district and
along the Sumida River.

Dodsworth was fascinated.

The duck was busy playing with
the kendama.

Except for the rickshaw incident, Dodsworth
was very happy with the duck so far.
The tour took them to the Imperial Palace.
They strolled through the lush East Gardens.
There were cherry blossoms everywhere.
Huge, colorful koi fish swam in a pond.
The duck loved the fish.

The duck jumped onto a bridge to see more fish.

"Please don't stand there," said the tour guide.

"Get down!" whispered Dodsworth loudly.

The duck turned to jump down.

He lost his balance.

He fell into the water.

"Help!" shouted the duck. "I can't swim!"

"That's absurd," said the guide. "You're
a duck."

Dodsworth knew the duck couldn't swim.
He went in and pulled the duck out of
the water.

The tour guide just shook his head.
The tour continued.

Dodsworth was soaked and he was
not happy.

"I knew it wouldn't last!" he said.

"I slipped," explained the duck.

"I don't care," said Dodsworth. "Any
more trouble, and no wagashi."

The duck felt bad.

They arrived at the Museum of the
Imperial Collections.
There were rooms of priceless treasures.
Dodsworth looked at the duck and the
kendama.
"I'll hold that," he said.
The duck handed him the kendama.

Dodsworth looked down at the duck.
"Now remember," he said. "If you're
good, wagashi. If you're not, no wagashi.
So just think about wagashi and you'll
be fine."
The duck tried to think about wagashi.

They walked by beautiful ancient bowls.
"Imagine Japanese emperors eating from
these very bowls," said the tour guide.
The duck imagined the bowls full of wagashi.
He felt like jumping into the imaginary
wagashi. Thankfully, he didn't.

They passed a hall of Japanese brush
paintings.

"These are sumi-e paintings," said the guide.

"Let's all try painting a tree. It's fun."

Everyone was given a brush, ink, and paper.

The duck had always wanted to play with ink.

"Remember," said Dodsworth, "wagashi."

Everyone made little brush paintings.

The duck kept thinking about wagashi.

He tried very hard not to spill any ink.

The paintings came out quite nicely.

Most of the paintings looked like trees.

The duck's painting looked more like a

cupcake.

Dodsworth gave the kendama back to the duck.

They walked through a quiet Zen garden.

The duck was tired.

He sat down on the grass.

He calmly played with the kendama.

"Your duck is very peaceful," said a lady.
Nobody had ever said that about the duck
before either.
"You should visit Asakusa," said the lady.
"The Sensō-ji temple is there. It is very serene."
Dodsworth thought that was a wonderful idea.

CHAPTER THREE

ASAKUSA

They took a taxi to the temple at Asakusa.

It wasn't as quiet as Dodsworth had expected.

It was very crowded, with dancers and food
and music everywhere.

The Sanja Festival was taking place.

It was a giant celebration.

Groups carried beautiful, ornate shrines
and wore bright, colorful costumes.

Taiko drummers were beating their drums.

The duck started tapping his feet to the music.

The duck began to sway back and forth.

He did a quick little spin.

"Remember," said Dodsworth, "wagashi."

The music was so loud, the duck didn't
hear him.

The duck started dancing with other folks.

"Don't disappear into the crowd," said
Dodsworth.

"Hey, look!" yelled the duck as he
disappeared into the crowd.
Dodsworth tried to run after him.
It was so crowded that he couldn't move.
"Wagashi!" he shouted to the duck.
Folks gave him a funny look.

The duck ran across a row of taiko drums.
The patter of his feet fit the music perfectly.
The crowd cheered.

"Don't encourage him!" yelled Dodsworth.
The duck grabbed a rope and swung over
the festival. The crowd cheered again.

"This won't end well," said Dodsworth.

The duck dove across a table.

He bumped into a game where everyone
was catching goldfish.

Water splashed all over the place.

That group didn't look very happy about it,
but the crowd kept cheering.

The duck flipped over the crowd
and bounced off an awning.
The crowd cheered even louder.
Dodsworth couldn't see the duck anymore.

The duck jumped over a statue and bumped
into some folks carrying a shrine.
They almost dropped the shrine.
That was not good.
The crowd stopped cheering.
The music stopped completely.

Dodsworth made his way through the crowd.

He saw the duck sitting on the ground.

Everyone was staring at the duck.

Dodsworth dropped his head.

"I knew it," he said.

The duck stood up.

He walked over to a little girl.

He held out the kendama.

"I think this is yours," he said.

CHAPTER FOUR
SAYONARA

The girl's father said, "This is her favorite toy. Her grandfather made it. We thought it was gone forever. You have done a great thing. *Domo arigato.* Thank you very much." He bowed to the duck.

The duck bowed back.

Everyone cheered again.

"That was amazing!" said Dodsworth. "All that
flipping and jumping and sliding. Wow!"
"It was the only way I could get through the
crowd," said the duck.
"Why didn't you just fly?" asked Dodsworth.
"Never learned how," said the duck.
Dodsworth laughed.

"You're something else," said Dodsworth.
"I mean, think about everything you just
did."
The duck thought about everything he
just did.

The duck lifted the kendama.

He popped the little ball into the cup.

"Arigato!" he said.

There was a brief moment of silence.

But then, as the moon rose over Mount
Fuji, you could hear Dodsworth laughing
all the way down in Yoyogi Park.

A cake knocked the lady's hat off, a roll
landed on Dodsworth's nose, and the duck
fell and crushed the rest of the wagashi.
Dodsworth couldn't believe it.
He just looked at the duck and asked,
"What could you possibly have to say now?"

A lady walked in with a tray of wagashi
and a beautiful red kendama.
Dodsworth smiled.
The duck jumped up to thank her.
He knocked the tray and everything
went flying.

The duck seemed quiet.

"Everything okay?" asked Dodsworth.

"Fine," said the duck.

The duck never used the word "fine."

Ten minutes later, there was a knock

at the door.

They took a taxi back to the hotel.

When they stepped out of the taxi, the duck
bowed to the driver.

He also bowed to the folks at the front desk.

Dodsworth loved that.

They went to their room.

He thought about the rickshaw, the kendama,
the sushi, the East Gardens, wagashi, the
museum, the kendama, the brush paintings,
the Sanja Festival, the kendama.
He really liked that kendama.